Make Way for August

Mamie Moore
AR B.L.: 3.0
Points: 0.5

Make Way for August

Mamie Moore

PHOTOGRAPHS BY BRUCE CAINES

NEW WRITERS' VOICES
Literacy Volunteers of New York City

NEW WRITERS' VOICES® was made possible by grants from: An anonymous foundation; The Vincent Astor Foundation; Booth Ferris Foundation; Exxon Corporation; James Money Management, Inc.; Knight Foundation; Philip Morris Companies Inc.; Scripps Howard Foundation; The House of Seagram and H.W. Wilson Foundation.

ATTENTION READERS: We would like to hear what you think about our books. Please send your comments or suggestions to:

The Editors
Literacy Volunteers of New York City
121 Avenue of the Americas
New York, NY 10013

Printed in the United States of America.

97 96 95 94 93 92 91   10 9 8 7 6 5 4 3 2 1

First LVNYC Printing: March 1991

ISBN 0-929631-36-6

New Writers' Voices is a series of books published by Literacy Volunteers of New York City Inc., 121 Avenue of the Americas, New York, NY 10013. The words, "New Writers' Voices," are a trademark of Literacy Volunteers of New York City.

Cover designed by Paul Davis Studio; interior designed by Barbara Huntley.

This book was edited with the cooperation and consent of the author.

Executive Director, LVNYC: Eli Zal
Publishing Director, LVNYC: Nancy McCord
Managing Editor: Sarah Kirshner
Publishing Coordinator: Yvette Martinez-Gonzalez

LVNYC is an affiliate of Literacy Volunteers of America.

ACKNOWLEDGMENTS

Literacy Volunteers of New York City gratefully acknowledges the generous support of the following foundations and corporations that made the publication of WRITERS' VOICES and NEW WRITERS' VOICES possible: An anonymous foundation; The Vincent Astor Foundation; Booth Ferris Foundation; Exxon Corporation; James Money Management, Inc.; Knight Foundation; Philip Morris Companies, Inc.; Scripps Howard Foundation; The House of Seagram and H.W. Wilson Foundation.

We deeply appreciate the contributions of the following suppliers: Cam Steel Die Rule Works Inc. (steel cutting die for display); Boise Cascade Canada Ltd. (text stock); Black Dot Graphics (text typesetting); Horizon Paper Company and Manchester Paper Company (cover stock); MCUSA (display header); Delta Corrugated Container (corrugated display); J.A.C. Lithographers (cover color separations); and Offset Paperback Mfrs., Inc., A Bertelsmann Company (cover and text printing and binding).

For their guidance, support and hard work, we are indebted to the LVNYC Board of Directors' Publishing Committee: James E. Galton, Marvel Entertainment Group; Virginia Barber, Virginia Barber Literary Agency, Inc.; Doris Bass, Bantam Doubleday Dell; Jeff Brown; Jerry Butler, William Morrow & Company, Inc., George P. Davidson, Ballantine Books; Joy M. Gannon, St. Martin's Press; Walter Kiechel, *Fortune*; Geraldine E. Rhoads, Diamandis Communications

Inc.; Virginia Rice, Reader's Digest; Martin Singerman, News America Publishing, Inc.; James L. Stanko, James Money Management, Inc. and F. Robert Stein, Pryor, Cashman, Sherman & Flynn.

Thanks also to Joy M. Gannon and Julia Weil of St. Martin's Press for producing this book; Ann Heininger for her editorial and interviewing skills; Natalie Bowen for her thoughtful copyediting and suggestions; and Helen Morris for her dedication and helpful contributions at so many stages of the book.

For producing the photography for this book, we are very grateful to Ed Susse. Our thanks also to the cast of MAKE WAY FOR AUGUST:

Mamie: Michelle Hurst; **Takeenah:** Beth Brice; **Dover:** Troy Barrett; **Ticket Agent:** Nancy Allen.

Our special thanks to those who helped us with the photography: Rita Katcher; Leslie Price of The Boyar-Prosky Agency; Jack Byrnes, General Manager, American Airlines, MacArthur Airport; Bradley Ringhouse, Town of Islip, Long Island; Valerie Barrett; Mattie Wilks; and Eartha Thompson of the Cornerstone Baptist Church, Brooklyn.

Our thanks to Paul Davis Studio and Myrna Davis, Paul Davis, Jeanine Esposito, Alex Ginns and Frank Begrowicz for their inspired design of the covers of these books. Thanks also to Barbara Huntley for her sensitive design of the interior of this book and to Ron Bel Bruno for his timely help.

And special credit must be given to Marilyn Boutwell, Jean Fargo and Gary Murphy of the LVNYC staff for their contributions to the educational and editorial content of these books.

The author wishes to thank Delores Nowlin and Marilyn Collins.

CHAPTER

1

Last July, I went
to Wilmington, North Carolina,
to visit my mother.
I took Takeenah,
my youngest daughter,
with me.

My mother had
two guinea pigs.
I did not like them at first.
But the longer I stayed,
the more I liked them.

Takeenah had never seen
or held guinea pigs before.
She fell in love with them.

My mother said
Takeenah could have one
of the guinea pigs.
She could take it home
to New York.

We had to give it a name.
The summer before,
we got a cat
and named it July.
We decided to stick with tradition
and named the guinea pig August.

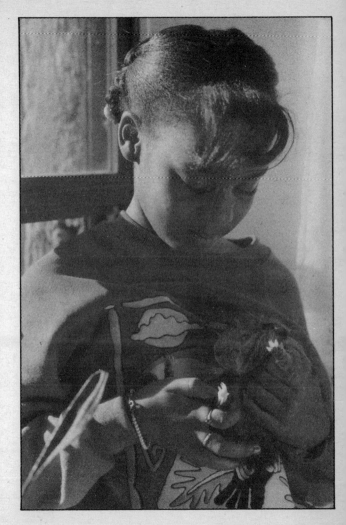

It was time to go home
to New York.
I knew it was expensive
to ship an animal
on an airplane.
So I decided to hide August
in a shoe box
and carry her on the plane.

I put the shoe box
in Takeenah's backpack.
And off we went
to the airport.

CHAPTER

2

While I was checking in,
Takeenah peeked in the backpack.
She came over
and pulled on my sleeve.
"Mom! Mom!"
she said.

"What do you want?"
I asked.

"August is out of the box!"
she told me.

I told Takeenah to be quiet.
I didn't want the woman
at the counter
to find out about August.
I was so scared
I could hardly write my name
on the luggage tags.

Takeenah and I
went into the ladies' room.
And that was when I learned
that a guinea pig
can chew through *anything*.

August had chewed her way
right out of the shoe box.
I put her back
into the box.
Then I stuffed some things in
to cover up the hole
she had chewed.

I was all right
until we got to
the metal detector.

Then I got scared.
But the backpack with August
went through
and nobody stopped us.
Boy, I was so glad.

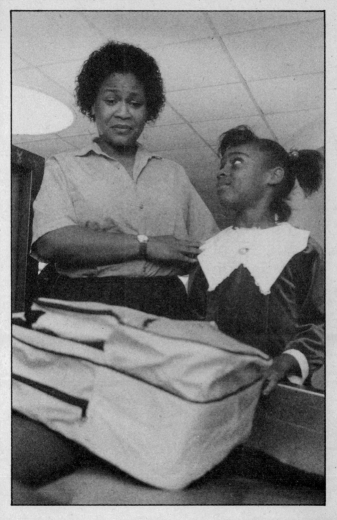

We went to the waiting area.
Takeenah went to the window.
"Momma, come here,"
she called.
"Look, are those our bags?"

I said,
"They look like ours."
Then I went across the room
to sit down.

I stared across the room
at the backpack
under Takeenah's feet.
I was so worried about August
getting out of the shoe box
that I did not hear the call
to board the plane.

When I looked up,
all the passengers were gone.
I went over to the woman and asked
"When is the flight to New York
leaving?"

She looked out the window
and said,
"There she is on her way now."

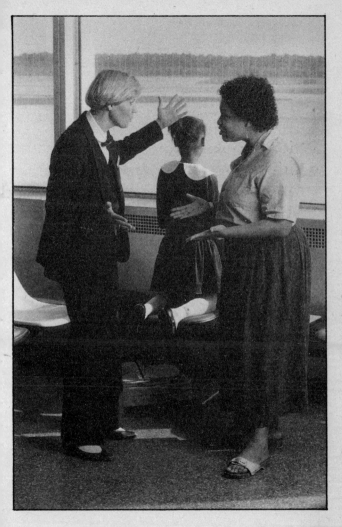

I was very upset
that I had missed the flight.
I told the woman
I had to get home
and asked her what could be done.
She said she would try to get us
on the next flight.
It would leave in two hours.

Now I was really scared.
One, I had to sit in the airport
with a guinea pig
for two hours.
Two, I had to call home
and let them know
I had missed my plane.

I called home.
My son, Dover, answered the phone.
I asked for my husband, Moore.
Dover said he had gone
to the airport
to meet my plane.
I knew I was in trouble.

Takeenah was hungry.
We went to the food counter
and I bought her a frank.

August smelled the food.
We heard her trying to get out
of the shoe box.
I decided it would be safer
to sit and wait outside.

I opened the backpack
and took August out
so she could get some air.
Takeenah shared the frank with her.

31

CHAPTER

4

It was finally time
for our plane to leave.
We went back inside
and got on board.
At last, we were on our way home.

We settled down with the backpack
under the seat in front of us.
I unzipped it a little
so I could keep my eye
on the shoe box.
Everything was fine
until the stewardess came
with our meal.
August went wild!

I pulled the pack onto my lap
and peeked in the box.
I could see
those beady little black eyes
staring at me.
August was chewing and wiggling—
anything to get at that food.

I knew what we had to do.
We broke up our dessert cookies
and fed them to August.
As long as she had food,
she was happy.
I prayed we would not
run out of food.

The flight only took two hours
but it felt like six!

Moore was waiting for us
when our plane landed.
But he was pretty angry
that we had missed the first flight.

It was almost 3:00 A.M.
when we got home.
I was one happy and tired woman.

CHAPTER
5

When we got upstairs,
we opened the backpack.
August had chewed up
most of the shoe box.

I let her out
to see her new home.
August had been born down South
but she was now a City Guinea Pig.

We bought a cage for August.
We put her in the cage
at night.
But during the day,
she had the run of the house.

We all loved August,
even our cat, July.

August went everywhere.
She got into the cabinets
and dresser drawers.
She hid under the beds.

One day, we were sitting
in the living room
and saw August climb
halfway up the curtains!

At first I didn't understand
that guinea pigs chew *everything*.

August loved to go
into Dover's room.
His clothes were always
all over the floor.
August liked to chew his socks—
and anything else lying around.

I told Dover,
"I bet you'll pick up your clothes
now."
That made me laugh very hard.

"Momma, it's not funny,"
Dover said.

"Yes, it is.
You won't pick up your clothes
for me
but you will for August."

CHAPTER
6

One morning, I was in the kitchen
making breakfast.
Takeenah came in,
looking frightened.
I asked her what was wrong.

She said,
"Momma, August won't move."

I asked her why.
She was very scared and said,
"I do not know."

"Go and get August,"
I told her.

Takeenah brought August
into the kitchen.
I looked at August.
Then I looked at Takeenah
and asked her what happened.
I said,
"This time you better tell me
the truth."

"I stepped on her,"
Takeenah sobbed.
"My room was dark when I got up.
I didn't see her."

I knew then that August was dead.

I had never been in a situation
like this before.
I wanted to punish Takeenah
for killing August.
It was a natural reaction.
Inside, grown-ups are children too.
When someone hurts
what you care about,
you want to hurt them back.
And I had loved August too.

But I knew that would be wrong.
I said to myself,
"Okay, Momma,
you better get yourself together."
When it comes to children,
mothers have to know
how to control themselves.
Mothers have to be more grown-up
than children.

Takeenah was crying.
I was trying hard
not to cry myself.
But I did not want Takeenah
to feel guilty.
She was only seven years old.
I did not want it
on her conscience
that she had killed
something she loved.
I did not want my child hurt
for a guinea pig.

It was hard to know
what to say or do.
I took Takeenah in my arms
and told her it was all right.
It had been an accident.
It was not her fault
that she didn't see August
in the dark.

Takeenah asked me
what I was going to do
with August.
I told her
we would give August
an incinerator burial.

52

I put Takeenah back in bed.
She was exhausted from crying.
I told her
I would get her
another guinea pig.

We all miss August so much.

A DISCUSSION
WITH THE AUTHOR
Mamie Moore

**By Ann Heininger, Staff Member,
Literacy Volunteers of New York City**

I first met Mamie Moore two years
ago at LVNYC's annual Evening of
Readings. She had just read her
story—aloud and on stage—to an
audience of almost 1,000 people. It
didn't seem to scare Mamie that she
shared the stage with six well-known
authors who were also reading their
stories. Nor that the president's wife,
Barbara Bush, was on stage.

Mamie really won the audience with
the story of August, the guinea pig.
First she had them rolling in the aisles,
then she had them in tears.

Now that Mamie was a graduate of LVNYC, I hadn't seen her in a while. So I was looking forward to meeting her again. We met at one of LVNYC's learning centers. We were joined by Nilsa, a student who wanted to talk with Mamie about her story.

We enjoyed talking about Mamie's story. It made us think about being parents and it made us remember our own childhoods. We're sure the story made you think about some of these issues too.

Our discussion follows. You may want to read different parts of it at different times. You may want to have it read aloud in a small group where you can discuss it.

ANN: How did you come to write this story, Mamie?

MAMIE: Before I went down South, I told myself whatever happens, I'm going to write about it. Lord knows there's a lot of interesting stuff happening in my hometown. If I could write it all down in a book, I could be a millionaire.

NILSA: So how did you decide on the guinea pig story?

MAMIE: Once Takeenah had the guinea pig, I started to think of a way to get it home. I thought it would make a nice little story. But when I got to the airport and all these crazy things happened, I *knew* I had to write it down.

ANN: What do you think makes a story good?

MAMIE: Well, first of all, humor. And it's important to keep the reader's attention. When the guinea pig is making a fuss at the airport, you wonder if we will get home. When the animal dies, you wonder what will happen to the child. When I read a good book, it grabs me and I have to know what happens next. I can't put it down. I keep on reading.

ANN: Why is humor important?

MAMIE: There's so much sadness nowadays. As far as I'm concerned, I want to laugh at something. I want to feel good and I want people to make me laugh. Sure, something sad might have happened but give me something funny that happened too. Something good always happens with the bad.

NILSA: This story is happy and sad. When it ended, I felt bad because the child was sad.

ANN: I was touched because you sympathized with Takeenah rather than coming down on her.

MAMIE: I'll tell you, raising kids ain't no picnic. You've really got to put your mind to it, really think clearly, if you're going to do it right. My kids do some crazy things. It's not easy to know when and how to discipline your kids.

NILSA: My son came home crying the other day. He and his friends were pushing another friend who uses a wheelchair up a hill. They lost control of the wheelchair. The little boy fell out. My son felt terrible but I didn't want to punish him because it was an accident. We were both relieved to find out the little boy was all right.

MAMIE: See, if something like that happens to a kid and he comes to you laughing, you know he doesn't care and he doesn't care about others in his heart. You have to straighten that child out. But if he comes to you upset and sorry and you yell at him, you could leave a mental scar. A lot of parents don't realize that when they verbally abuse a child, it stays with that child all through his life.

ANN: Have you ever been sorry you punished one of your children?

MAMIE: Of course. My son. He could never sit still when he was little. He

59

was always running around. He broke up so much of my furniture—not intentionally—but still, I'd get so mad I wanted to beat him. Then I'd think, Why do I want to beat him for breaking something that I can put back together? He's 17 now and he's still very active. But I've changed a lot. I wish I knew then what I know now.

ANN: What has changed about you?

MAMIE: Being able to read and write has changed me a lot. I used to get so aggravated with myself and my kids. When you can't read, you think everybody is talking about you, you think everybody is better than you. I've learned that ain't true. I also know now that there are no experts. Look at the newspapers and television. They tell the same story in different ways, they can't all be right. I think more of myself now that I can read and write and that means I'm better with my kids. I don't get so frustrated and we don't give each other such a hard time.

60

ANN: I thought, in the story, you did just the right thing, taking Takeenah in your arms. Do you remember any times your parents did just the right thing?

MAMIE: When I was young, I had a baby that was stillborn. It tore me up. All I did was cry. When I came home from the hospital, Momma gave me a teddy bear and said, "Here's your baby, right here. When you want to cry, you hold this." She helped me through that difficult time.

NILSA: My relationship with my parents wasn't as good as that. But you can learn how to treat your kids from others and by what wasn't done for you. I've seen parents treat their children like precious gold. That's what I try to do. I try to treat my kids like precious gold.

MAMIE: Right.

TO OUR READERS

If you have a piece of writing you would like us to consider for a future book, please send it to us. It can be on any subject; it can be a true story, fiction or poetry. We can't promise that we will publish your story but we will give it serious consideration. We will let you know what our decision is.

Please do not send us your original manuscript. Instead, make a copy of it and send that to us, because we can't promise that we will be able to return it to you.

If you send us your writing, we will assume you are willing for us to publish it. If we decide to accept it, we will send you a letter requesting your permission. So please be sure to include your name, address and phone number on the copy you send us.

We look forward to seeing your writing.

The Editors
Literacy Volunteers of New York City
121 Sixth Avenue, New York, NY 10013

NEW WRITERS' VOICES

A SERIES OF BOOKS BY ADULT NEW WRITERS

Calvin Miles, WHEN DREAMS CAME TRUE, $3.50

Mamie Moore, MAKE WAY FOR AUGUST, $3.50

Theresa Sanservino, CAN'T WAIT FOR SUMMER, $3.50

FROM MY IMAGINATION, An Anthology, $3.50

SPEAKING FROM THE HEART, An Anthology, $3.50

SPEAKING OUT ON HEALTH, An Anthology, $3.50

SPEAKING OUT ON HOME AND FAMILY, An Anthology, $3.50

SPEAKING OUT ON WORK, An Anthology, $3.50

TAKING CHARGE OF MY LIFE, An Anthology, $3.50

To order, please send your check to Publishing Program, Literacy Volunteers of New York City, 121 Avenue of the Americas, New York, NY 10013. Please add $2.00 per order and .50 per book to cover postage and handling. NY and NJ residents, add appropriate sales tax. Prices subject to change without notice.

WRITERS' VOICES

Kareem Abdul-Jabbar and Peter Knobler, *Selected from GIANT STEPS*
Rudolfo A. Anaya, *Selected from BLESS ME, ULTIMA*
Maya Angelou, *Selected from I KNOW WHY THE CAGED BIRD SINGS and THE HEART OF A WOMAN*
Peter Benchley, *Selected from JAWS*
Ray Bradbury, *Selected from DARK THEY WERE, AND GOLDEN-EYED*
Carol Burnett, *Selected from ONE MORE TIME*
Mary Higgins Clark, *Selected from THE LOST ANGEL*
Avery Corman, *Selected from KRAMER vs. KRAMER*
Bill Cosby, *Selected from FATHERHOOD and TIME FLIES*
Louise Erdrich, *Selected from LOVE MEDICINE*
Alex Haley, *Selected from A DIFFERENT KIND OF CHRISTMAS*
Maxine Hong Kingston, *Selected from CHINA MEN and THE WOMAN WARRIOR*
Loretta Lynn with George Vecsey, *Selected from COAL MINER'S DAUGHTER*
Mark Mathabane, *Selected from KAFFIR BOY*
Gloria Naylor, *Selected from THE WOMEN OF BREWSTER PLACE*
Priscilla Beaulieu Presley with Sandra Harmon, *Selected from ELVIS AND ME*
Mario Puzo, *Selected from THE GODFATHER*
Ahmad Rashad with Peter Bodo, *Selected from RASHAD*
Sidney Sheldon, *Selected from WINDMILLS OF THE GODS*
Anne Tyler, *Selected from THE ACCIDENTAL TOURIST*
Abigail Van Buren, *Selected from THE BEST OF DEAR ABBY*
Tom Wolfe, *Selected from THE RIGHT STUFF*
SELECTED FROM CONTEMPORARY AMERICAN PLAYS
SELECTED FROM 20th-CENTURY AMERICAN POETRY

Books are $3.50 each. To order, please send your check to Publishing Program, Literacy Volunteers of New York City, 121 Avenue of the Americas, New York, NY 10013. Please add $2.00 per order and .50 per book to cover postage and handling. NY and NJ residents, add appropriate sales tax. Prices subject to change without notice.